Get a Haircut

Written by Caleb Burroughs
Illustrated by Jacqueline East
Cover illustrated by Louise Gardner

Louis Weber, C.E.O., Publications International, Ltd.
7373 North Cicero Avenue, Lincolnwood, Illinois 60712

Ground Floor, 59 Gloucester Place, London W1U 8JJ

Customer Service: 1-800-595-8484 or customer_service@pilbooks.com

www.pilbooks.com

Permission is never granted for commercial purposes.

p i kids is a registered trademark of Publications International, Ltd.

ISBN-13: 978-1-4127-9184-7
ISBN-10: 1-4127-9184-7

8 7 6 5 4 3 2 1

pi kids® **publications international, ltd.**

Hi! My name is Claire. I have a twin brother named Aaron. This morning when Aaron and I were getting ready for the day, our mommy came into the bathroom.

"Your hair is looking a little shaggy," she said. "You two need haircuts!"

I guess it had been a while since we'd had our hair cut.

Mommy drove us downtown to the barber shop. It's called Toni's Cut 'n' Curl, and it's a place where only kids can get their hair cut.

"That looks like a candy cane!" I said.

"That is a barbershop pole," said Mommy.

"Come on, you two," said Aaron. "Let's go inside!"

A smiling lady led us into the shop. "My name is Toni," she said. "This is my salon."

Toni led Aaron and me to two really cool chairs. The chairs had levers that let her pump them up until they were really tall.

Then she put a special cape on each of us. "This is called a smock," she said. "It will keep the hair off of your clothes."

"I'm Jean-Luc. I need to shampoo your hair," a smiling man said. "It will be clean and easier to cut when it's wet."

He leaned Aaron's chair way, way back. His head rested over a special sink. Jean-Luc put shampoo in Aaron's hair and worked it into a lather. Then he rinsed away the bubbles.

"It's so clean!" Jean-Luc said.

Once Jean-Luc had washed our hair, he began to cut mine.

"Just relax, my dear," he said. "I am going to give you the most fabulous haircut!"

After combing my hair until it was straight, he started to snip away with his scissors.

"Just a bit here," he said. "And just a bit there. You are looking marvelous!"

After Jean-Luc cut my hair, I looked into all the mirrors that were around the shop. I could even see Aaron in one of them!

"What's making that buzzing sound?" Aaron asked.

"These are clippers," said Jean-Luc. "I'm using them to trim the hair on your neck."

"Hee hee!" Aaron laughed. "Those clippers are tickling me!"

Once Jean-Luc was finished cutting our hair, it was time to take a look.

"Going down!" said Jean-Luc. He pushed a pedal on the chair with his foot. With a whoosh, the chair lowered to the floor.

Toni gave us each a mirror. "What do you think?" she asked.

"My hair looks great!" said Aaron. "Claire's does, too!"

When we were all done Mommy was waiting for us.

"Claire, you look beautiful," she said. "And Aaron, you look very handsome."

I agree! I love haircuts!